Jen Jeffrey Billington & Friends

Copyright 2025

Faith Words Publishing

ISBN # 978-1-959369-18-9

In loving Memory of Ava Watkins, WATCH Board of Directors 1984-2024

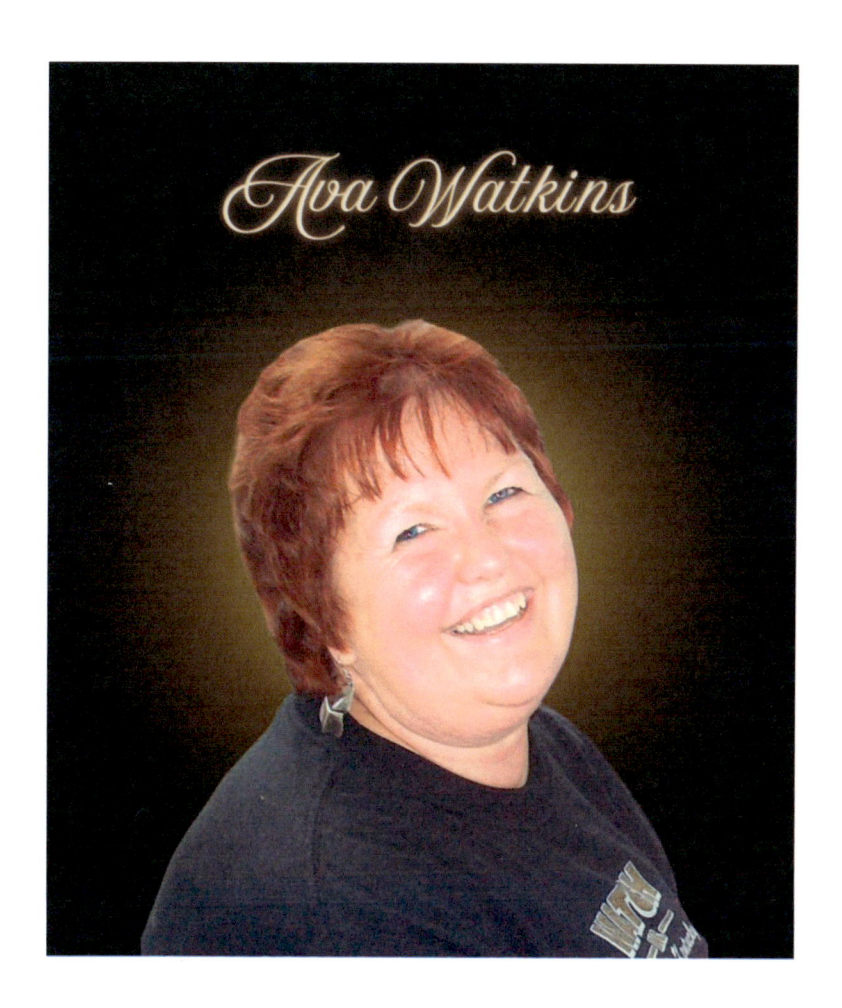

WATCH Me!

Introduction

As an author, I am all about the written word. I love words! I love how words can lift someone's spirit. Our local community's Work Activities Training Care for the Handicap program for adults is called WATCH. I refer to the members as my friends and often refer to them as my special friends.

Without the confusion or political correctness, I focus on the *heart*. God has *my* heart, my husband's heart, the hearts of parents and caregivers, and, of course, our special friends. They *are* special to us not because they have special needs but because their hearts are so pure and full of joy—that is very special! We learn so much from them.

My husband Jason and I lead a class for our special friends at church. It is the GSP class (God's Special People), and they love knowing they have special gifts to give this world. When we are around our friends, we are reminded of the truth God teaches in His Word about showing grace to others, forgiving each other, and caring. In a busy world, it is good to be reminded to slow down and simplify the things we make so difficult.

When I began teaching a class at WATCH, I found how much my new friends there love words, too. *Disclaimer:*

WATCH Me!

Some of our participants are under the State's guardianship, and we cannot use their names. Some of our authors will only have their initials by their work.

We hope that our friends' unique abilities to raise awareness of the simple acts of kindness, love, and grace (as we were once taught) will keep you focused on what is most important.

" ...the greatest of these is love.'

Chapter One

Verbal Book

In our first class, we did an ice-breaker exercise before our first writing session: we wrote a verbal book by writing it aloud. Two of our friends are blind, and I didn't want them to leave the class if they thought they couldn't participate. It was essential to begin with this verbal exercise until they felt comfortable. I started with a sentence, and the rest of the class added to it.

After everyone had a turn, we read the story back, and they giggled with glee! I think at first, they didn't understand how to continue the story from the person before them, so some of them said the same thing.

Towards the end, they got the hang of it and laughed so much, hearing the story we created together. Our special friends teach *us*. I loved that they could laugh at themselves and had joy working together.

WATCH Me!

"Once upon a time in a land far, far away..."

Julia - *"I was driving and singing away..."*
Jennifer - *"And I was driving a van..."*
A.L. - *"And I drove a Chevy Impala to a dance."*
Kelly - *"And I was singing..."*
Crystal - *"And I took my dog for a walk..."*
Stephen - *"And I was on stage singing at the Grand Ole Opry..."*
A.S. - *"And I danced away..."*
Jordan - *"I was watching college football..."*
Floyd - *"I was a prison guard and taking cell phones away..."*
A.M . - *"And I talked to my girlfriend on my cell phone..."*
Tracy - *"I was sleeping..."*
Ruthie - *"And I was laying down..."*

I asked how we should end the story, and Crystal held her arms out and said, *"And this is what we did in a land far, far, away."*

WATCH Me!

ABOUT ME

Jordan Lowe
I live with my father.
My favorite color is Purple.
My favorite animal is a dog.
My favorite pastime is watching TV and watching the Special Olympics.
How I like to help others - I don't know.

Stephen Norsworthy

I live with a guardian.
My favorite color is pink.
My favorite animal is a cat named Blue.
My favorite pastimes are music, such as Vince Gill, Grand Ole Opry, bowling, and shopping at Walmart. I also like CDs.

A.L.

I live with my caregiver, Adam.
My favorite color is red.
My favorite animal is a kitty. I love it, and hold it, and kiss it. Her name is Lucy.
My favorite pastime is drawing trains.

WATCH Me!

I help others by working at Zaxby's, wiping off tables, taking trays, and calling the names of people to pick up their meals.

A.M.

*I live with my caregiver.
My favorite color is black.
My favorite animal is a dog.
My favorite pastimes are playing baseball and watching TV -Walker Texas Ranger.
The way I help others is by opening doors and mowing.*

Ruthie

*I live with my mom.
My favorite color is red.
My favorite animal is "Marcy," a dog.
My favorite pastime is to help Sheila do stuff; I also like pickleball.
I help others by getting Tim and Sheila's vitamins, walking Ruby, and counting money.*

WATCH Me!

Floyd Mendosa

*I live with a caregiver, Kathleen.
My favorite color is blue.
My favorite animal is a Chihuahua.
My favorite pastime is reading and watching YouTube videos.
I like to help people by supporting blind people.*

A.S.

*I live with a caregiver, Morgan. My favorite color is baby blue.
My favorite animal is a dog.
My favorite pastime is singing.
How I help others is praying and showing respect.*

Kelly

*I live with my caregiver and with dogs, a rabbit and a hamster named "Chip," and my dogs' names are "Copper" and "Jake."
My family has six cats and one dog named Gizmo.
I like to watch TV and movies.
My favorite color is pink.*

My favorite pastime is doing Special Olympics, softball, bowling, and bocce ball.

Zach Thomas

*I live with my mom and dad.
My favorite animal is a dog. A black lab named Shadow.
My favorite color is blue.
I listen to music, watch TV and play games.
I help others by asking them what they need, and then I help them.*

Tracy Marceau

*I live with my sister Vicki, brother-in-law Derek, and nephew Dominic. Dominic plays football. I like to spend time with my niece Ava, Conner, and their dog Scout. My favorite animal is Sparky, my dog.
My favorite pastime is watching TV, Hocus Pocus, and Hocus Pocus II.
My favorite color is purple.
My friends are Crystal, Ruth, Kelly, Julia, Kirby, and Justin.
I like to help people with work and to help the staff pass out lunches.*

Crystal Estes

I live with a family home provider. I call them my mom and dad. I have been with them since 1996.
My favorite color is pink.
My favorite pet is a Pug named Honey.
My favorite pastime is watching TV and walking my dog. I do bowling, softball, and basketball for Special Olympics. I also love pickleball.
I help kids do crafts.

Julia Wages

I live on my own but on my caregiver's property.
My favorite color is pink.
My favorite animals are dogs and cats.
My favorite pastime is listening to music, sleeping, and watching movies. I play bowling with Special Olympics.
How I help people is just to listen if they have a problem.

WATCH Me!

Jennifer Worthington

*I live with my sister.
My favorite color is purple.
My favorite animal is a dog.
My favorite pastime is being on my iPad.
I help others by talking to them and caring about them.*

T Bone (Tommeall)

*I live with my caregiver, Cynthia.
My favorite color is Saphire.
My favorite animal, even though I like cats and dogs, I have to say, are birds.
My favorite pastime is watching things on the internet and playing card games.*

Tequila

*I live with my caregiver, Tierra Robertson.
My favorite color is purple. I have two favorite animals. Cats and dogs. There are two cats on the front porch, one inside, four dogs out in the back yard and one inside. My favorite pastime is listening to music, watching my Madea movies, and singing.*

To help others, I just listen to them and talk to them. I work for Pella, assembling products.

Cheeseburger
I live with Carey and Rhonda. My favorite color is blue. My favorite animal is a dog. My dog is named Rex. My favorite pastime is to watch TV. I like watching Andy Griffith. I help others by putting stuff up and helping them out.

Phillip

I live with my caregivers, Wanda and David. My favorite color... one of them is pink, and another is light blue. My favorite animal is a rabbit. They are cute and cuddly. I also like carrots.
My favorite pastime is Bowling, and I like to play games. I like Bingo. To help others, I tell them they look nice.

WATCH Me!

I AM DIRVERING A CAR
I AM GO TO AT R-ED

MURRAY ROCKETS BOWLING
IN MURRAY KENTUCKY
I AM GOING T BOWLING

Drawing by A. L.

WATCH Me!

Phillip

Chapter Two

Imagine Heaven

In class, we discussed Heaven and how we would be given perfect bodies one day. The writing prompt on this day was, "What would you like to do when we are all in Heaven with our perfect bodies? What job would you like to have?"

I got a little misty-eyed, with much joy, when T-bone gave me his answer.

While practicing illustration, I planned to help Floyd with his drawing. He is blind. He wanted to draw San Fransisco Bay, with a bridge over it and a train. I put a blue crayon in his hand and told him what color we used. I placed my hand over his and guided it to make waves: " Swoop, swoop, swoop... do you feel the waves, Floyd?" He smiled a big smile.

Floyd - *"When I am in Heaven, I want to be a train Engineer. To sit in the back and make the train go. In one direction and then turn the switch when it changes."*

A.S. - *"When I am in Heaven, I will rejoice. I want to be a preacher and talk about God."*

Kelly - *"When I am in Heaven, I will direct a choir."*

A.B. - *"When I am in Heaven, my job will be to wash windows."*

Ruth - *"In Heaven, I will dance and sing."*

Tracy M. - *In Heaven, I will be an Artist."*

Tracy gave Ruthie the picture she drew. I took a picture first before she did. It made Ruthie so happy.

Stephen N. - *"In Heaven, I will sing!"*

A.L. - *"I want to be a storyteller... about trains. A CSX Deisal."*

M.H. - *"When I'm in Heaven, I want to make poetry and read it to others."*

Crystal - *"I want to play softball and sports in Heaven."*

A.M. - *"In Heaven, I will see my best friend, Michael Cross."*

Zach T. - *"In Heaven, I want to sing."*

T Bone - *"My life is pretty perfect already, but I'd like to be a writer when I'm in Heaven."*

It touched me when T-bone said his life was pretty perfect already. He has Cerebral Palsy, which has affected his speech and walking, among other things, yet he smiled when he said this. He meant it. May we all have hearts like T Bone.

WATCH Me!

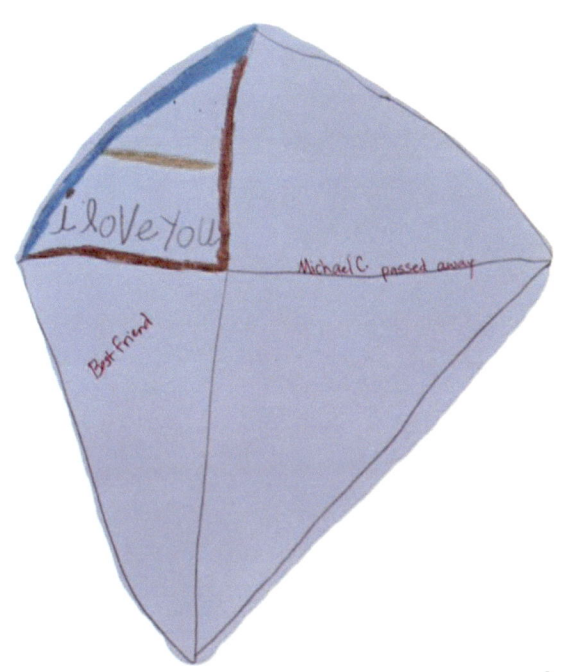

A. M.

WATCH Me!

GOD IS LOVE

A. L.

WATCH Me!

A. L.

WATCH Me!

A. L.

WATCH Me!

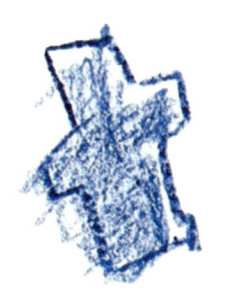

A. S.

WATCH Me!

A. B.

WATCH Me!

Crystal

(Drawn by M. H.)

WATCH Me!

Floyd

28

WATCH Me!

Kelly

WATCH Me!

Ruth

WATCH Me!

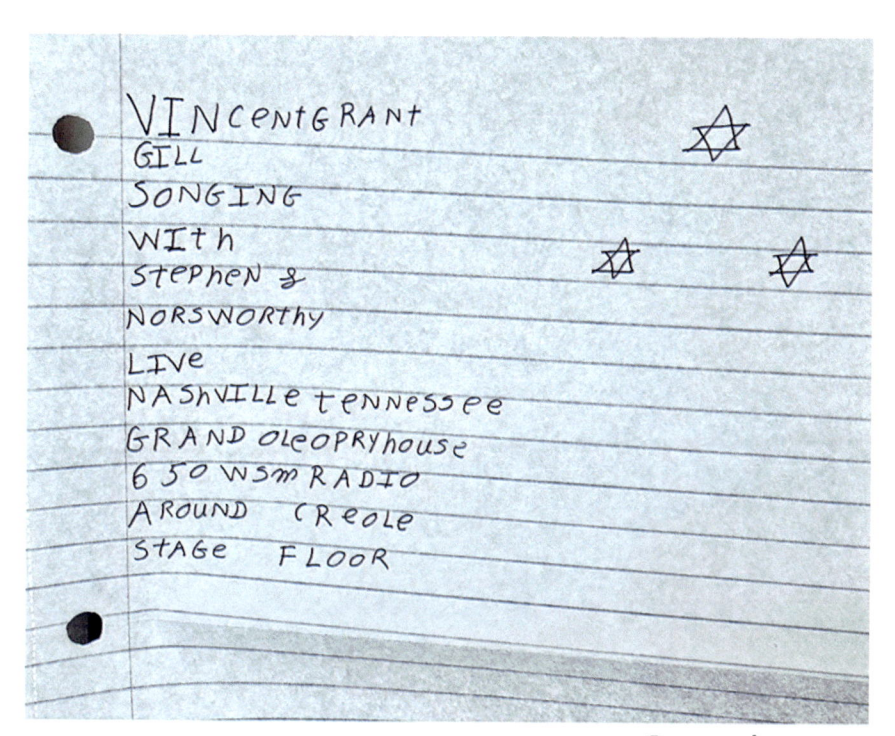

> VINCent GRAnt
> GILL
> SONGING
> WIth
> stephen &
> NORSWORthy
> LIve
> NAShVILLe tennessee
> GRAND OLeOPRYhouse
> 650 WSM RADIO
> AROUND CReole
> STAGE FLOOR

Stephen

WATCH Me!

Stephen

WATCH Me!

Tracy

WATCH Me!

Zach

(Cruise Ship)

Chapter Three

Change the World

For this prompt, we went around the room discussing what we would do to change the world. Knowing that class members sometimes have difficulty thinking of something, I prepared a beach ball with ideas written on it. I had an assistant with me that day.

Perry Prince attends my husband Jason's and my Sunday School class at Hardin Baptist. Perry is tall, slender, and moves like the wind. He was the perfect helper to chase the ball when it dropped and to toss or hand it to others when it was their turn.

This was a fun activity for our class. Some of the class read ideas from the ball, and others thought of their own.

Floyd – *"I would make rails for trains across the world."*

Crystal – *"I would give someone a compliment."*

A. S. – *"I would be humble and kind."*

M. H. – *"I would write about Captain Blackbeard."*

A. M. – *"I would pick up trash on the ground."*

A. L. – *"I would be kind. And I also would tell Darth Vader to act his age."*

Jennifer – *"I would clean my room."*

Tracy – *"I would love with all my heart."*

T Bone – *"I would be grateful."*

Zach – *"I would forgive people and forgive myself."*

Ruthie – *"I would smile."*

Stephen – *"I would smile."*

A. B. - *"I would be good to others, be happy, smile, and love one another as myself, and help people that need help."*

WATCH Me!

Illustrated by M. H.

WATCH Me!

Illustrated by Ruthie

WATCH Me!

PiCk UP trash on ground

♥

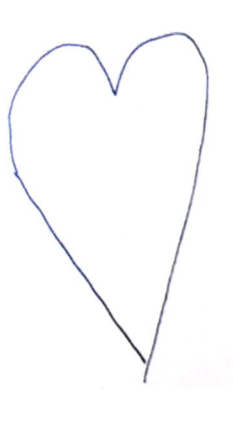

Illustration by A. M.

WATCH Me!

Illustration by Jennifer W.

WATCH Me!

BE KIND TO GOD
GOD IS LOVE

Illustration by A. L.

WATCH Me!

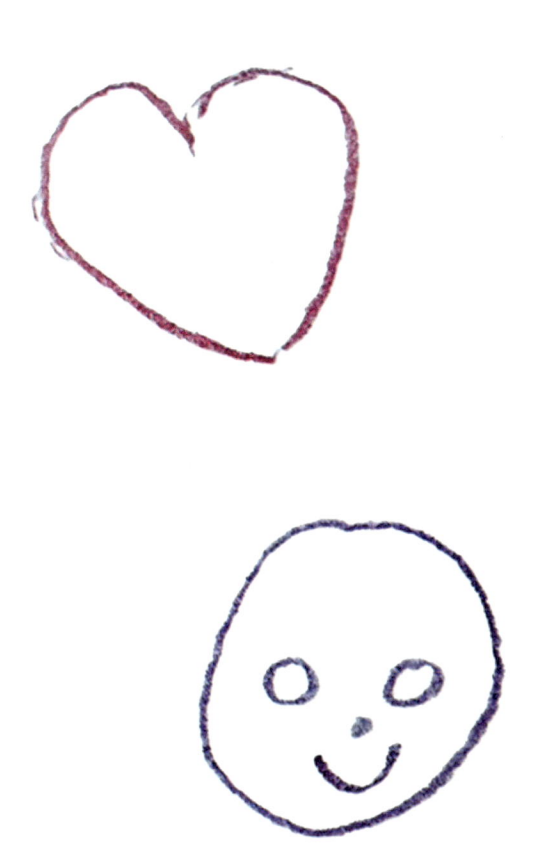

Illustration by A. B.

WATCH Me!

Illustration by Kelly B.

Chapter Four

Poetry

The class learned about poetry and how we use words to describe our thoughts and feelings using our senses. For a writing prompt, I brought a stuffed toy cardinal. The class also learned about rhyming, rhythm, and pattern. The two members, who do not have a sense of sight, held the bird first, and I asked them to describe how it felt and sounded. They loved the chirping sound it made.

Each of them got to describe the bird using their senses, and then we wrote a poem about it together on the board and worked on rhyming.

Tequila

"It's soft. I feel his head, his eyes, and his beak."

Floyd

"Velvety. Its beak is cute. I feel it's head. It has a soothing sound."

A.B.

"It feels soft. Its beak is pointy. It is a bright red color."

Jennifer

"It makes a noise. Cheap, cheap!"

A.M.

"It tickles (rubbing it on his face). It makes a noise like a bunny. I feel it's nose – it's like a carrot."

Tracy

"It has a pretty sound and a nice tail. It has black eyes, and it's red. My aunt has a cardinal shirt."

Julia

"It's a red bird. Its color is bright, and it has dark black eyes. It's hair feels weird. It makes a whistling sound."

Kelly

"It has a happy chirping sound. It's soft and fuzzy."

"A.L."

"It has a pretty sound. And it reminds me of the Mayfield Redbirds and the St. Louis Cardinals. And it's beautiful."

"M.H."

"It's red. It cheaps, and its tail is feathery."

T Bone

"It's hair is, I'll say, buck-wild!"

Zach

"It's soft. It has happy chirping. It has a red beak and black eyes."

Stephen

"I feel it in my heart."(He pushed the sound). Its name is a Cardinal. It's red, and its hair is fuzzy."

Crystal

A Cardinal is a special bird. It is red, and I love to watch them fly. It feels soft and has like a chirping sound. He is also the State bird.

After describing the bird, we had time for only a short poem in which they collaborated together.

Cardinal

The Cardinal reminds us of someone sweet.

He makes a sound that goes, 'tweet, tweet.'

His body is uniquely soft,

And his name is Mr. Croft.

WATCH Me!

howdose it look pretty
howdose it feel sweet
howdose it sound good
3 HIS DOLY UNI GUFIY

A.L.

howdose it look pretty
howdose it feel Bick
howdose it sound

Tracy

howdose it look Red
howdose it feel soft
howdose it sound happy

Kelly

WATCH Me!

Poetry
Cardinal make believe
They are red and black
They are feathery
They chirp like small birds

If I were a cardinal
I would have red and black
feathers. I have a beak that eat
insects and berries and seeds
I would ruffle my feathers
and go to sleep in the nest
Laura Croft the cardinal
The cardnal reminds us as
sweet. Then tittweets

M. H.

M. H.

WATCH Me!

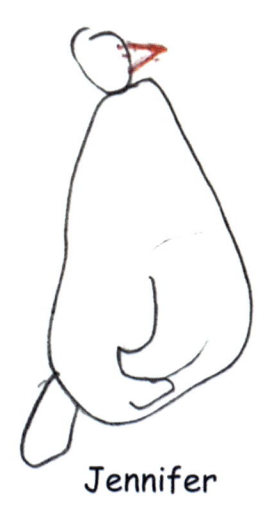

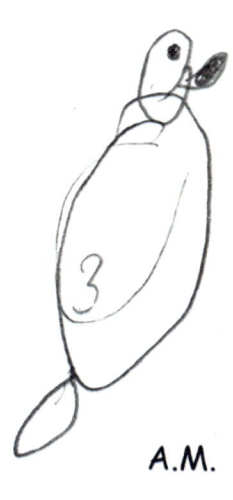

Jennifer

A.M.

WATCH Me!

Floyd

Stephen

Julia

Zach

52

Chapter Five

Friendship

Our writing prompt during this session was about friendship. How we feel about someone we think of as a friend and how they are a friend to us.

A.B.

Crystal Estes is a friend of mine. She is nice, smiles, and says good things. We like to talk on the phone, and we celebrated my birthday.

A.L.

My girlfriend Debbie. She loves me. She is a good person. I like to wait on her and do stuff for her.

Kelly

"I have a friend in Julia. I can tell that she cares. And my friend Belinda helps me and always encourages me, and so does my caregiver Kayla. She encourages me to do things I don't think I can."

T Bone

Julia is probably my best friend. I have known her for a very long time. She is my funny friend and makes me laugh."

Floyd

"I had a good friend, Cliff Key. He has passed away. He always gave me good drinks and had a hilarious personality."

Stephen

"I have a friend, Samuel Arnold. His mom is a preacher, and I like to sing with her. She goes to Tennessee."

Tequila

"Amanda is a friend of mine. We started WATCH about the same time a few years ago. We cut up. She likes to hear me sing. She calls me Mama. We are angels to each other."

Julia

"Tommeall (T Bone) is a friend of mine. He is protective of me. He makes me smile and laugh. Sometimes, I help translate for him if someone can't understand him. I have known him for a long time. We have writing in common."

A.M.

"My friends are Lily and JD. They are my caretakers and go out to eat with me. We spend time together."

M.H.

"William Jones is my friend. We talk about trains. And Crystal Estes is my best friend. She is my girlfriend. She is sweet to me and is a good dancer."

Crystal

"My sister Jessica and I have a friendship. We are like two peas in a pod. I help her at the house and go to my niece's ball games. M.H. is my friend. He and I go out. One of the things I love about him is his laugh. Sometimes you think he's crying, but he's laughing. He treats me nicely. I also have two best friends - Julia and Kym."

Chapter Six

Pain

This class was not an easy one. Our authors thought about a time that brought them pain. I wanted them to think about how they coped, what helped them through their pain, and how it impacted their lives. This exercise was to show that everything isn't always happy, but we get through hardships together. After opening up a few wounds, we closed them with good thoughts. Mostly, they are joyful, but everyone in this world will experience troubled hearts. Jesus said, "Take heart; I have overcome the world."

Tequila

"It hurt me that a family member was in a fire. She was covered in fire, and her skin fell off. Mother had pulled a sheet from her bed and got the fire out. She was delirious. I was scared at first. I saw a bright light."
(Tequila is mostly blind).

Floyd

I lost someone. My sister-in-law passed away. I have to deal with it every year.

T Bone

Well, I have been through a lot in my life. But there is one thing that is very painful. My mom passed away in 1996. She was my best friend. I am very independent and stuff, but the thing about me is that even having a mom who passed away and a brother who passed away, I can't waste my life. Know what I mean? And that gives me the strength to move forward."

A.M.

"I lost two dogs. That made me mad. It hurt my next-door neighbor, too. He cried."

Tracy

"My mom passed away. I saw my mom in her hospital bed. That was scary. I cried. I helped my mom. I still do what she taught me, washing my hands and cooking."

A.B.

"My mom and dad got divorced, my dad got remarried, and my mom moved to Texas with my sister. My brother died of bone cancer. I still talk to my dad, but it's hard when my sisters argue."

Ruthie

"I lost my dog, Marcie. She was outside and hadn't been found. It makes me nervous. My mom cannot find Marcie. It wasn't my fault. I look at her picture, and it makes me feel better."

Jordan

"I lost a parent. My mother. She died of Lupus. And my pet Bassett hound Molly died. She ran into the road and got run over. Mom and Molly are in Heaven. My mom beat breast cancer twice, but the Lupus got her. I miss my mom and Molly every day of my life.

Stephen

I have been in the hospital. I had surgery. I got my eyes fixed and my dentist. I had people pass away. My uncles, aunts and cousins. My cat Blue makes me feel better. She licks my nose every morning and night."

Crystal

A sad thing happened to me was my dog got run over. My vet called me when I was on the bus going to basketball. I called my mom and dad, crying. My dad buried him. My brother had Pugs, and I got one. My other dog was outside and escaped, but I keep Honey inside. She is my baby."

Kelly

"I lived in a group home, and they had to close it down. And that was the hardest thing. Everything in my life changed."

Zach

One of our dogs passed away last year. His name was JJ. We used to lie down together and play together. Now, I play with my dog Shadow.

Michael

"When I was a kid, I broke my arm. I fell from the slide in the park. I had a bloody nose. Another thing that hurt, I lost my grandmother. And my stepdad had a heart attack. My watch got broken, and that made me mad. It had the date on it. I also fell running to second base and scraped my knee and face. But I keep on playing."

Julia

"I was at WATCH when I found out my dad passed. My dad was very sick, and it

hurt me when I found out he passed away. I cried my eyes out, but God helped me go through the pain. My friends helped me go through a tough time.

A.L.

When I lost my stepmom, my grandma, and my grandpa, I would be sad around Christmas. I miss them all. When you lose loved ones, it hurts. Another thing that hurts is my birth mom, who tried to drown me when I was about four years old. I decided to walk away from it cause it was too much on me. We need to move on from our pain."

A.L. goes to my church, and on Mother's Day of this year, we were outside waiting on the bus after church, and he told me he was sad about what his mom did. He had the biggest crocodile tears fall from his pretty blue eyes. My heart hurt for him. A.L. is in his 60s, but I felt like a mama to him and hugged him tight. Some of our friends have gone through unimaginable pain, but how they teach us through their resilience.

WATCH Me!

Writing in their books.

One of our dogs passed away and it made us realy sad on March 28th 2023 but me and my family had to remind ourselfs that our pet did'nt want us sad but we cride we were sad.

One time when I was a kid I broke my arm once, I fell from the slide the top of the slide in a park. It
I lost my grandmother when I was 30 something or late 20s I miss her alot.
couple weeks ago my stepdad had a heart attack
I was in Softball this past year I had a watch broke I been run to 2nd base and fell face first and skid my right knee.

my dad died he was very sick so it hurt me when I founded out that he passed away but I cried my eyes out. but god help me go thraugh the pain. Kirby and other people like family and friends help me through the tough time I was A WATCH when I founded out my dad passed Kirby brought me in the bosses office & every staff was there with me and my boyfriend and that when I foundout & ALSO my mom called & told me.

When I was growing up I didn't have much childhood. I was taken away from my real mom and DAN. I move to from to different fosters home, IN PADUCAH then I move to Murray, was IN foster homes. But then I found the perfect family. I call them mom and DAN. And their kids I call my Brother and sisters, I have been with them since 1996. I love them dearly. They took me in when I don't have nowhere to go. They got me a pug. They love me as their own.

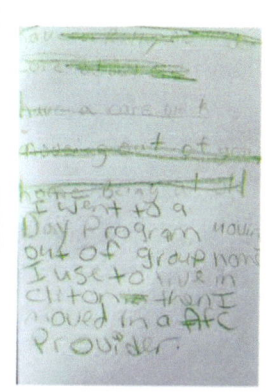

I went to a Day program moving out of group home I use to live in Clifton then I moved in a AFC provider.

Chapter Seven

Childhood

Our writing prompt for this chapter was supposed to be fun, take us back to being kids, and pull out fun memories from childhood. I understand some of our friends didn't experience happy childhoods, but I tried to pull out thoughts where they could have a good memory. Perhaps they remembered being outside as a child and feeling the warm sun on their face. Tequila closed her eyes and smiled at the thought. Maybe they remember a food they loved as a kid, like cotton candy.

Some of their stories were verbal, while others were written. My husband Jason and I told them stories of our childhood, and they got a kick out of the one where I pinched Jason when we were babies. Every day has a story. It's my goal to help others see the good in each day.

T Bone

"This story is about a big clock! My mom woke me, telling me it was time for school. I didn't want to get up. She said, 'Boy, you better get up, or something else is gonna wake you up!' And the train came by and was so loud, it shook the house! It went, 'WOO! WOO!'"

T Bone gestured with his arm as if pulling on a train whistle. He's such a good storyteller. I hope you will look for his book "No Ordinary Guy," on Amazon.

A.L.

"I used to watch Lost In Space. That was a good show. Dr. Smith was a bad boy. He was a criminal. Also, when I lived with my aunt, I ate ice cream and had cake for my birthday."

Kym

"I like hanging out with Crystal and Julie. All the time. And Special Olympics."

Phillip

"I liked going to church. My mother cooked good. I liked Turkey and Dressing. I liked going to the store and shopping. I liked to sleep."

A.B.

"I liked skipping, Hopscotch, running, and Special Olympics. I liked catching the bus. I used to beat Crystal to the bus. I've known her for a long time."

A.S.

"When I was little, I loved butter beans, corn, and country ham."

Stephen

"When I was little, I watched Lassie and made mud pies. I liked to watch my mommy cook. Me and my brother used to play school."

Ruth

"I had good memories. At Christmas time, Santa brought me clothes. I liked spending time with my family."

A.M.

"When I was a kid, I bit my sister on the nose. I watched Rescue 911. I liked seeing the firefighters and ambulances and the police catching bad guys. I busted my nose once on a cop car."

Kelly

"I liked to swing. I liked to swim and go for walks. I liked to play outside and play games."

Tracy

"Watching Chicago Bears with my parents. I liked catching fireflies. I like yellow flowers. I was happy with my family. I liked Thanksgiving and going to Derek's."

Julia

"When I was little, I got baptized and asked God to be in my heart. When I got older, I played bowling in Special Olympics. I loved it so much. When I was little, I used to fight with my sister, but now we get along."

M.H.

"When I was a toddler, I lived in Marion. I had a crib and put my hand through the holes and it got stuck. I couldn't get it out. I cried, and my grandmother tried to get my hand out. Another memory we had good cooking when my grandmother made homemade biscuits and Chicken and Dumplings."

Crystal

"When I was growing up, I didn't have much of a childhood. I was taken away from my real mom and dad. I moved to different foster homes in Paducah and then to Murray. But then I found the perfect family. I call them Mom and Dad, and their kids are my brother and sisters. I have been with them since 1996. They took me in when I had nowhere to go. They got me a pug. They love me like their own. I remember our first Christmas together. They got me lots of clothes and a TV. I am very active in church now, working with kids. I do Special Olympics and go lots of places with my new family. I didn't get to do that in the past. I get to stay with my foster sister a lot. This family treats me like their daughter."

Chapter Eight

On Their Own

This chapter ends our book with the offerings that a few of our class members handed me and what they wanted to add to the book.

"M.H." handed me several handwritten pages, and when I glanced at them, I saw that they looked like song lyrics copied from the internet until I looked closer. The more I read, the more I smiled and giggled.

Enjoy these fun writings straight out of M.H.'s head.

WATCH Me!

Offerings by M.H.

Captain Blackbeard Medley Featuring Rock You

We will, we will rock you. We will, we will rock you. Biggy, biggy man, went to the farm with red clothes to feed the bull with BBQ sauce, and the bull ran over me like a bull dozer-man. Oh yeah, man! We will, we will rock you. We will, we will rock you.

Biggy, biggy, can you see when the world hypnotizes you? Biggy. Biggy, can you see when the world hypnotizes me? We will, we will rock you. We will, we will rock you.

Hit the road jack. Don't come back no more, no more, no more, hit the road jack, don't come back no more – Waz up? We will, we will rock you. We will, we will rock you.

WATCH Me!

Ahoy, Matey! I'm Captain Blackbeard, and I've sailed the seven seas all day long in New York-Jersey. Where I go, I don't know! Yo, ho, ho, and a bottle of rum. We will, we will rock you. We will, we will rock you. Sing it again! We will, we will rock you. One more time! We will, we will rock you. That's all, folks. No animals were harmed during the making of the medley.

Blackbeards Halloween

Ahoy, you Mateys! I'm Count Blackula. I've flown the seven skies throughout the night, where I go; staying away from the light sky. Yo, ho, ho, and a pint of blood.

Ahoy, you Mateys, I am Wereblackbeard. I ran the sven meadows of the woods throughout the night, where I go, howling the full moon. Yo, ho, ho, and a bottle of Elixer. Howl.

Ahoy, you, Mateys! I'm the Mummy Blackbeard. I sleep in the seven tombs in the pyramids, where I go, being wrapped up in life. Yo, ho, ho, and a bottle of gauze.

Ahoy, you, Mateys! I am Dr. Blackbeard. I work the seven labs to make a potion, to make me Mr. Black, where I go, being the nutty professor, Blackbeard style! Yo, ho, ho, and a bottle of serum to turn me back.

Ahoy, you Mateys! I'm Mario Blackbeard. I've traveled the seven kingdoms in the Mushroom Land, stopping the evil King Bowser, where I go; saving Pirate Princess Peach. Yo, ho, ho, and a chest of gold coins.

Santa Blackbeard Medley Featuring Funky Music

Na na na na na, hey, hey, goodbye. Na na na na na, hey, hey, goodbye. Hey, hey, hey, hey, hey, hey Macho, macho man, I want to be a macho man. Na na na na na, hey, hey, goodbye. Na na na na na, hey, hey, goodbye. Play that funky music, white boy. Play that funky music, right. Play that funky music, white boy. Dance and boogie and play that funky music till you die. Na na na na na, hey, hey, goodbye. Na na na na na, hey, hey, goodbye.

Ahoy Mateys! I'm Santa Blackbeard. I sleigh the seven skies all night long in the North Pole, where I go, delivering treasure. Ho, ho, ho, and a bottle of eggnog. Ho, ho, ho, Merry Blackmas! Na na na na na, hey, hey, goodbye. Na na na na na, hey, hey, goodbye. Sing it again! Na na na na na, hey, hey, goodbye. Na na na na na, hey, hey, goodbye. One more time! Na na na na na, hey, hey, goodbye. Na na na na na, hey, hey, goodbye. That's all, folks! No animals were harmed while making this medley.

Saint Blackbeard Medley Featuring Bad Boys

I will put a spell on you because you're mine. I will put a spell on you because you're mine. Something strange in the neighborhood, who you gonna call? Ghost Busters! Something weird in your backyard. Who you gonna call? Ghost Busters!

I will put a spell on you because you're mine. I will put a spell on you because you're mine.

Bad Boys, Bad Boys, what you going to do? What you going to do when they come for you? Bad Boys, Bad Boys, what you going to do? What you going to do when they come for you?

I will put a spell on you because you're mine. I will put a spell on you because you're mine.

WATCH Me!

Ahoy, you Mateys! I'm Saint Blackbeard! I soared the seven rainbows in Irish Shamrock, where I go, finding pots of gold in Ireland. Yo, ho, ho, and a bottle of Irish Cream.

I will put a spell on you because you're mine. I will put a spell on you because you're mine. Sing it again! I will put a spell on you because you're mine. I will put a spell on you because you're mine. One more time! I will put a spell on you because you're mine. I will put a spell on you because you're mine. That's all, folks.

Chief Blackbeard Featuring Shake Your Bootie

Shake your bootie. Shake your bootie. Shake, shake, shake! Shake, shake, shake! Shake your bootie, yeah. Hey, hey, it is Phantom of the Opera. The Phantom of the Opera inside your mind. Shake your bootie. Shake, shake, shake! Shake, shake, shake! Shake your bootie, shake your bootie. Once again! Hey, hey, hey, it's Fat Albert! Na, na, na, have a good day, that's right! Na, na, na, have a good day, yeah. Shake, shake, shake! Shake, shake, shake! Shake your bootie! Shake your bootie!

Ahoy, you Mateys! I'm Chief Blackbeard. I rode the seven lands all night long in the vast desert, where I go, doing a rain dance. Yo, ho, ho, and a bottle of Wrisk. Shake, shake, shake! Shake, shake, shake! Shake your bootie! Shake your bootie! One more time! Shake, shake, shake! Shake,

WATCH Me!

shake, shake! Shake your bootie! Shake your bootie! That's all, folks.

All-Star Blackbeard

Ahoy, you Mateys! I'm Captain Blackbeard. I sail the seven seas all day long in New York, Jersey; where I go, I don't know. Yo, ho, ho, and a bottle of rum.

Ahoy, you Mateys! I'm Franken-Blackbeard. I flew the seven haunted-flying Dutchmen's ship all night long in Death Valley, where I go, spooking everyone. Yo, ho, ho, and a bottle of potion. Happy Halloween.

Ahoy, you Mateys! I'm Santa Blackbeard. I sleigh the seven skies all night long in the North Pole, where I go, delivering treasure. Ho, ho, ho, and a bottle of eggnog. Ho, ho, ho, Merry Blackmas!

Ahoy, you Mateys! I'm Cupid Blackbeard. I've flown the seven continents around the world, where I go, shooting heart-shaped arrows. Yo, ho, ho, and a bottle of Champagne. Happy Valentines!

Ahoy, you Mateys! I'm Saint Blackbeard! I soared the seven rainbows in Irish Shamrock, where I go, finding pots of gold in Ireland. Yo, ho, ho, and a bottle of Lucky Shamrocks.

The Finale

Ahoy, you, Mateys! I'm Sonic Blackbeard. I speed through the seven zones in Dr. Eggman land. Where I go. I collect emeralds, one for each zone. Yo, ho, ho, and a chest of rings.

Ahoy, you, Mateys! I'm Bowser Blackbeard. I took the princess from each of the seven castles. Where I go? Waiting for Mario. The time has come. Come get me, Mario. Yo, ho, ho, and a gold chest of treasure.

Ahoy, you, Mateys. I'm Crash Bandicoot Blackbeard. I've been through levels collecting gems and crystals. Where I go, eating mangos and beating Dr. Cortex. Yo, ho, ho, and away we go.

Ahoy, you, Mateys! I'm Blackbeard, the dragon. I flew the seven Kingdoms all over the world. Where I go busting treasure chests for gems. Yo, ho ho, and a very smooth sailing we go.

Ahoy, you, Mateys! I'm Michael J. Blackbeard. I've gone seven years in the future, past, and alternate present. Where I go, change the time. Yo, ho, ho, and a time machine we go.

Offerings by A. L.

"A.L." is a born illustrator. He loves to draw trains, fire engines, and cars. I have watched him work hard on a picture, and he always gives it away. He loves to give. When someone gets a picture from A.L., it's a treasure from his heart.

WATCH Me!

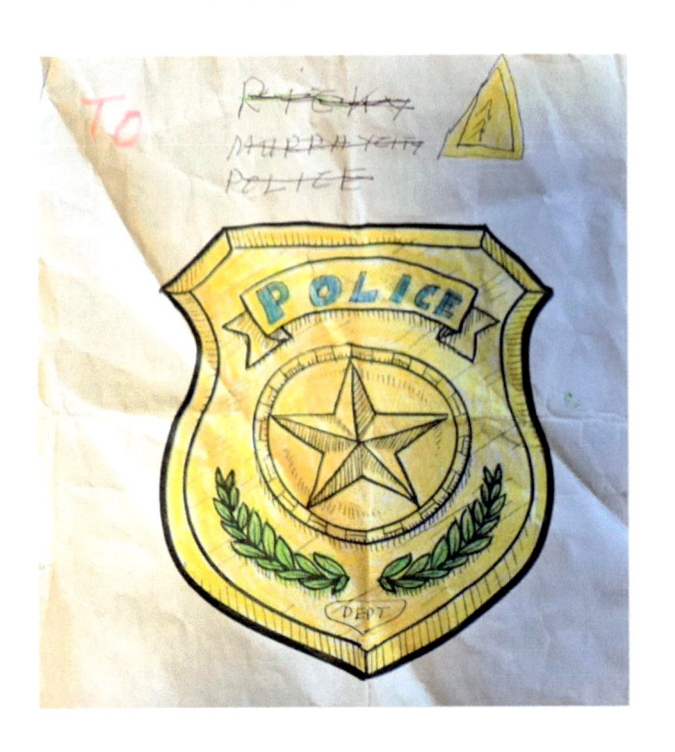

86

WATCH Me!

WATCH Me!

WATCH Me!

WATCH Me!

HARDING HURCH BAPTIST

HARDIN BAPTIST CHURCH

WATCH Me!

A. L.

Offerings by Crystal

How I Got My Pug

In February 2018, I had a Border Collie/Jack Russell that was run over. In April, I went to my brother's house.

I was sitting on the couch with all the Pugs. My mom took one outside, and then I went outside. Everyone told Mom that she needed to tell me what was going on. She said, "See that Pug that Dad is holding?" I said, "Yes." She said, "That is ours." I started crying.

Since then, my Pug has been my support and my favorite. Her name is Honey. She and I are buddies, and she sleeps with me. I take her walking, to the groomers, and I wouldn't trade her for the world.

She loves my boyfriend, too. She is now six years old and so precious. When I am sad, she senses that and gives me hugs and kisses. Without her, I would not have a little pet to play with and love.

WATCH Me!

My PUG

Honey and Me

Offerings by Julia W.

I have lived with Kirby and her family for five or more years. Now, I live on their property in a tiny home. It is awesome to have my own house.

Tre, Kaiden, and Addison are Kirby and Justin's kids. They are so sweet. I am glad I finally found a family that loves me and takes care of me if I need help—they are on it! I want to mention my mom and her husband, BoBo. We have been on vacation to Florida to see my mom and her husband, Raymond. My mom's name is Emma. My mom means a lot to me.

I have been with WATCH for five years and have made a lot of friends. The staff is also amazing, and I appreciate them so much.

Words from the Lead Author

Hanging out with our special friends at WATCH has brought Jason and me such joy.

The other day, I explained the difference between joy and happiness to **Julia.** I told her that I saw joy in her eyes. When I see pictures of her or watch her interact with others, she is expressive and eager to please. Her eyes light up. I told her this, and she told me something was going on right now that made her sad and told me about it. I told her I would help her pray about it. Then I told her sad things happened to me too. But no matter what happens, I still have joy. Happiness results from what happens, and there will be highs and lows in life, but joy is what's deep inside our hearts. Peace. Assurance of God's love.

On the day we worked on our last chapter, **Tommeall** and I talked about the book he has written that I am helping him publish. I had it formatted and edited, and it was ready on the publishing site. The only thing left to do was hit the button "PUBLISH." I pulled up the site on my phone and asked if he wanted to push that button. He pushed it, and I told him he was now a published author.

His smile said it all, but after writing his book for many years, I am sure it didn't seem real. It will. His book is being processed and soon to ship! The WATCH staff and I are eager to present it to him as we will be with this book for all our WATCH authors! Tommeall and I had time either before class or after to talk about his book, and it was an honor to help him make his dream come true. He has already begun writing a second book.

When I met **Tequila**, she joined the writing class on the first day and disappeared. Another day, I saw her in the cafeteria and went to talk to her. I told her that her friend Floyd was in the writing class, and I felt maybe she didn't stay because she could not see, but that I helped Floyd with his writing, and I would help her too if she would join us.

She liked that, so I asked her the "about me" questions to add to that section she had missed. Then, we chatted a little more and even sang a song together, "His Eye is on the Sparrow." I couldn't pick one friend that I was closer to than another. Each one is special to me because of their unique gifts and hearts.

A few have popped in and out of my class. **Kym** joined us on our last day, so I am still getting to know her, but she loves to write. As we wrote chapter seven, she wrote in a notebook I gave her, and it was very artsy and lined perfectly. She has better penmanship than me.

Floyd stayed with the writing class even though he was blind, and he seemed to enjoy talking about what we would write in our book. He has a wonderful smile and expression. I'm glad to be his friend. I loved peeling back the layers and finding a kind soul.

Ruthie came to most of the classes. I knew her when she used to attend our church. She is fun and loving. She has the cutest expression when she describes things.

Jason and I remembered **Tracy** when she used to attend our church, too. It's clear to see she is good friends with Ruth. Tracy recently lost her mother, and she has days when she pouts and talks about her mom. She gives great hugs.

Speaking of hugs, when one of our friends comes up to us and hugs us, it is so meaningful. One day, **Jennifer W**. came up to me and hugged me, and didn't let go. I didn't pull away or cue an end to the hug. I let her hug me for as long as she needed. It was about two minutes and made such an impact on me. Life gets busy, but I pray I always have two minutes for a hug.

M.H. is quiet and laid back but has a brilliant mind. He is funny and imaginative. Jason and I were amazed by his writing. When I found out that he and Crystal were an item, it made sense. **Crystal** is funny and likes to laugh, too. She sensed that I cared, so she confided in me about a few things and she has my cell number. She can text me any time. I love hearing from her. It is never a bother when our friends contact us.

A.L. goes to our church, and we love to hear him pray for our class. He prays from his heart, and oh, his heart is so big! He has such innocence and love. He is the most giving young man. Well, he is older than Jason and me, but his heart is so pure, like a child. He gives us pictures he draws and whatever item he has in his hand when his heart wants to show love.

A.B. is sweet and sensitive. She likes fairness and doesn't want anyone to get left out. She helped me when everyone would talk at once to let me know who had something to say if I missed it.

Jordan was only in two or three classes. I liked getting his goat when he told me he liked the Florida Gators, and I said, "Oh, I like the Vols." He smiled a mischievous smile. When he talked about the pain of losing his mom, I gave him ideas of how he could honor her. He was attentive and so sweet. I could not get his *author's picture*, but he is in a few candids. He is standing behind me in the top picture on page 109.

A.M. Is such a sweetie! I had just walked in the door and felt this arm around my neck hugging me! I turned to see his happy face. A.M. is also full of joy. I don't always understand his speech, but the more I am around him, I will. I take time to listen when he tells me something. He is so much fun. I love that he loves toys. Jason and I have toys, too. Never be embarrassed by your inner child, and be playful. It is a big part of having joy.

Kelly is a delight. She is helpful when I need her to tell me what a friend with unclear speech is saying or to help a classmate write or spell. She is energetic, and I like to hear her ideas.

Stephen is my quiet mouse. He is meek and soft-spoken. He usually has his headphones on when class begins, but the second I call on him, he perks up and has much to say. He likes hugs, too. And if anyone who reads this has a connection to Vince Gill, let him know that Stephen is his number-one fan.

Phillip joined the class toward the end. He goes to our church, too. He is quiet but always smiling and loves to talk to people when they talk to him. He plays the keyboard each Sunday and is polite and sweet.

"Cheeseburger" joined our class once, but I didn't get pictures of him. He also goes to our church. He loves to joke. I must share the character I made of him for our children's book series, Pengdom Living. We write stories about penguins, and some of them have special needs. I post jokes from the penguin characters on our Facebook page and create joke books. Cheeseburger was a fun penguin to create.

Another very polite friend is **Zach**. He is new to WATCH. Jason met him through Special Olympics, and he mentioned to Jason that he liked to write, so I contacted Zach's mom and told her about my class. Zach is clever and a good conversationalist.

Our friend **A.S.** has participated in class a few times but doesn't talk much. I am still getting to know her and want to hear her sing. We are excited to meet and learn about others at WATCH. The writing class could expand to more than just writing.

There is so much I want to share with our friends and mentor, encourage, and hang out with them. We truly love each one of our friends and are thrilled to be a part of WATCH and the special needs community.

Thank you to all my authors who joined me for this book! I love you all!

Jen

PHOTO GALLERY

Thank you to The Murray Insurance Agency for your *Quotes for the Community* donation and for purchasing copies of this book for all our authors.

WATCH Me!

WATCH Me!

WATCH Me!

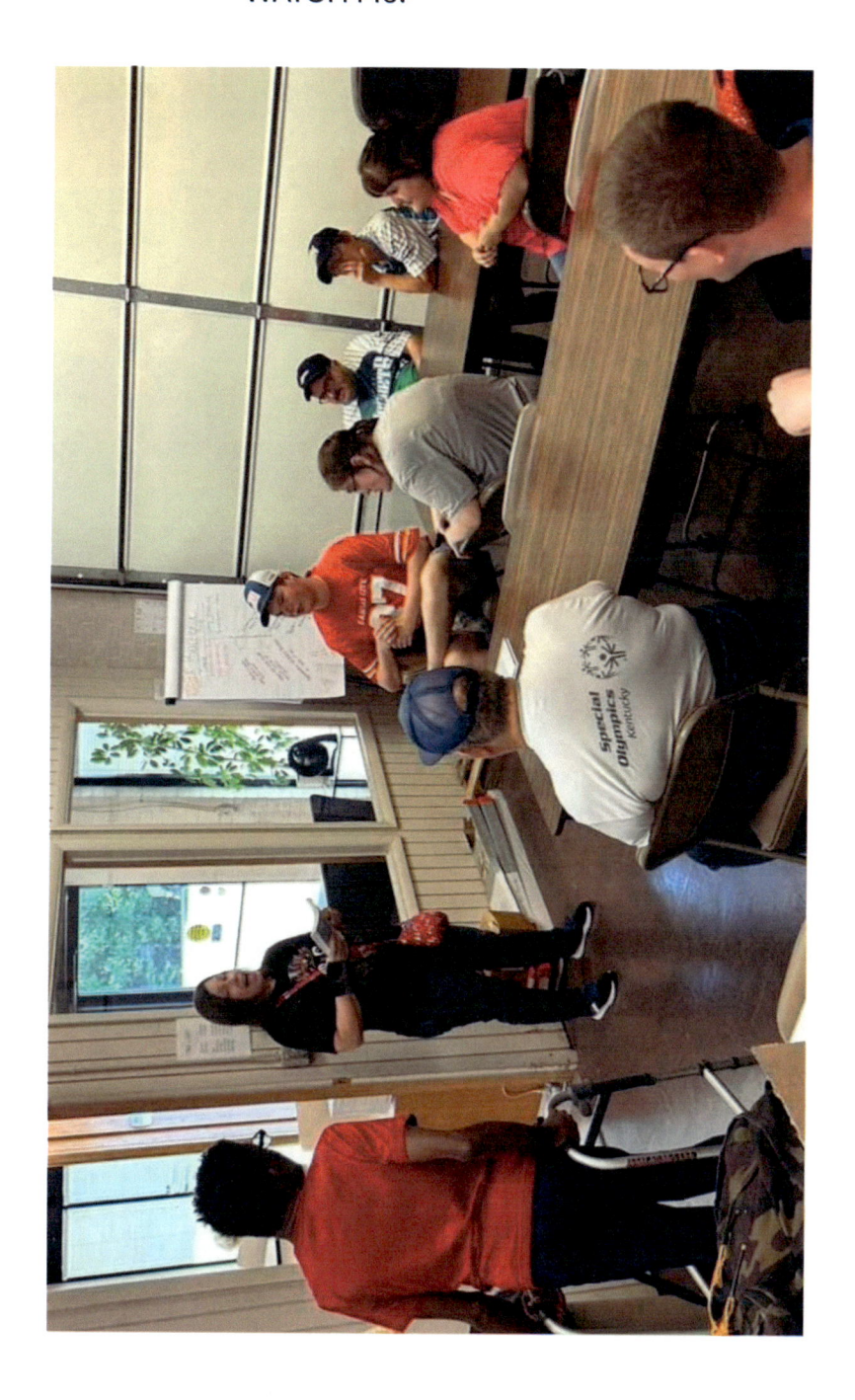

WATCH Me!

WATCH Me!

WATCH Me!

WATCH Me!

WATCH Me!

WATCH Me!

Our Authors

A.B.

Author: "A.B."

WATCH Me!

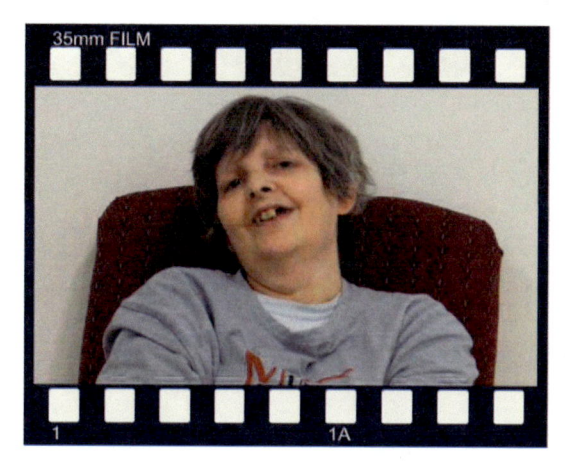

WATCH Me!

Julia

Author: Julia W.

WATCH Me!

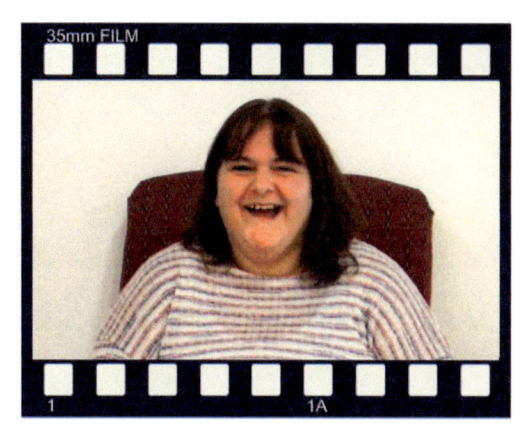

WATCH Me!

Kelly

WATCH Me!

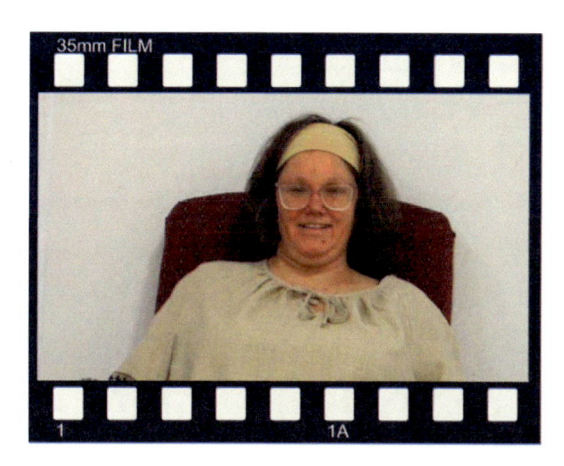

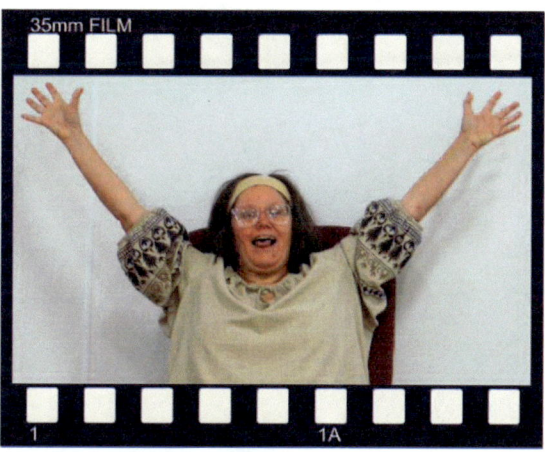

Crystal

Author: Crystal E.

WATCH Me!

WATCH Me!

M. H.

Author: "M.H."

WATCH Me!

WATCH Me!

A.L.

Author: "A.L."

WATCH Me!

WATCH Me!

Stephen

Author: Stephen N.

WATCH Me!

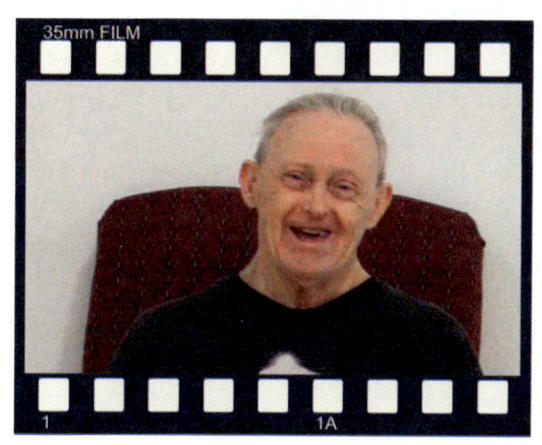

WATCH Me!

Jennifer

WATCH Me!

WATCH Me!

Zach

Author: *Zach T.*

WATCH Me!

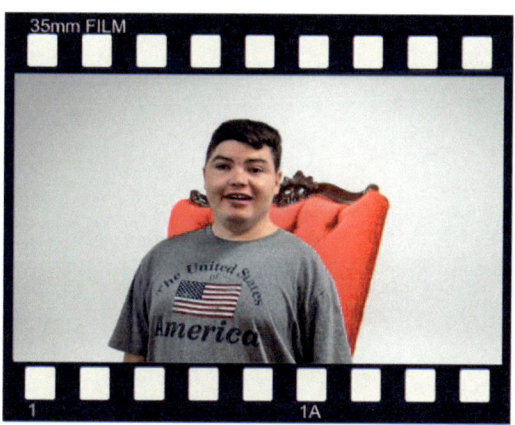

WATCH Me!

"A.S."

Author: "A.S."

WATCH Me!

WATCH Me!

Floyd

Author: *Floyd M.*

WATCH Me!

WATCH Me!

Phillip

WATCH Me!

WATCH Me!

Ruthie

Author: Ruthie

WATCH Me!

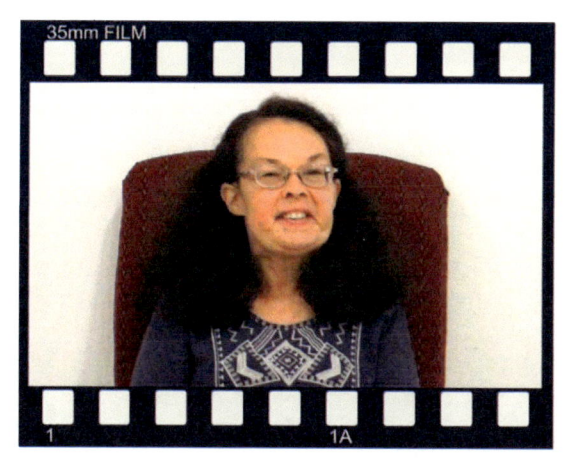

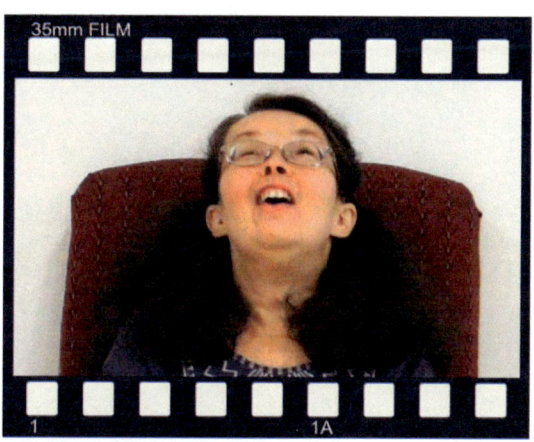

WATCH Me!

Tracy M.

WATCH Me!

A.M.

Author: "*A.M.*"

WATCH Me!

WATCH Me!

Kym Dickamore

WATCH Me!

WATCH Me!

Tommeall (T Bone)

WATCH Me!

WATCH Me!

WATCH members went around our community delivering Certificates of Appreciation to individuals, businesses, and organizations we have been associated with and who have supported us since WATCH was established in 1984. We are proud to have 40 years of history with each of you. ♥

~The WATCH Staff

WATCH Me!

BILL ADAMS CONSTRUCTION

BILL'S AWNINGS AND UPHOLSTERY

WATCH Me!

THE MURRAY LEDGER & TIMES

SUGAR CREEK BAPTIST CHURCH

WATCH Me!

THE MURRAY INSURANCE AGENCY

ALLISON HOWORKA

WATCH Me!

KIRKSEY UNITED METHODIST CHURCH

KNIGHTS OF COLUMBUS

WATCH Me!

THE CALLOWAY COUNTY PUBLIC LIBRARY

CALLOWAY COUNTY HEALTH DEPARTMENT

WATCH Me!

MURRAY ELECTRIC SYSTEM

CALLOWAY COUNTY FISCAL COURT

WATCH Me!

KIRKSEY BAPTIST CHURCH

MURRAY SUPPLY

WATCH Me!

WATCH Me!

PRINTING SERVICES OF MURRAY

OTTWAY SIGNS

WATCH Me!

Murray Fire Extinguishers

Mr. Gatti's Pizza

WATCH Me!

WATCH Me!

A special thank you to the WATCH staff for all your help and support to our favorite people!

WATCH Me!

Look for Tommeall's "No Ordinary Guy" book at Amazon Books under his pen name Andre W. Graham.

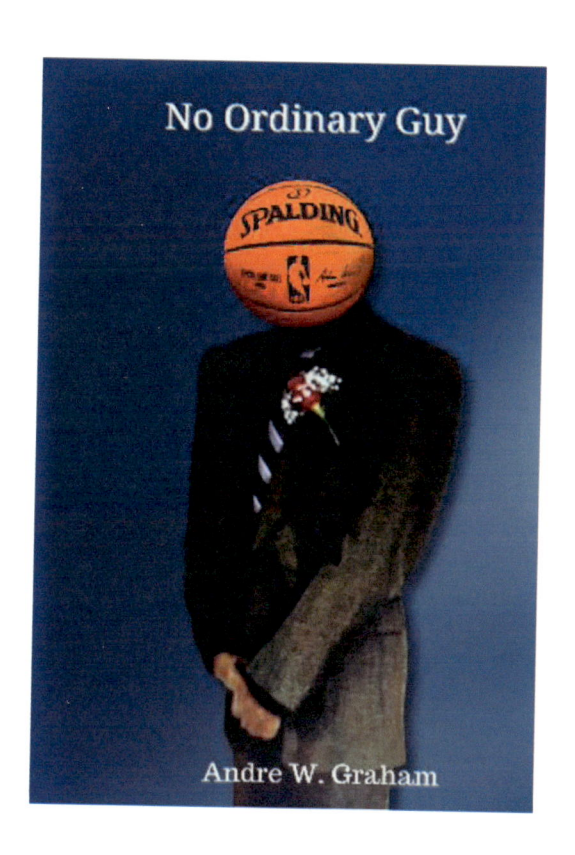

WATCH Me!

WATCH Me!

Made in the USA
Columbia, SC
14 February 2025